ABOUT THE BANK STREET READY-TO-READ SERIES

Seventy years of educational research and innovative teaching have given the Bank Street College of Education the reputation as America's most trusted name in early childhood education.

Because no two children are exactly alike in their development, we have designed the *Bank Street Ready-to-Read* series in three levels to accommodate the individual stages of reading readiness of children ages four through eight.

- *Level 1:* GETTING READY TO READ—read-alouds for children who are taking their first steps toward reading.
- *Level 2:* READING TOGETHER—for children who are just beginning to read by themselves but may need a little help.
- *Level 3:* I CAN READ IT MYSELF—for children who can read independently.

Our three levels make it easy to select the books most appropriate for a child's development and enable him or her to grow with the series step by step. The *Bank Street Ready-to-Read* books also overlap and reinforce each other, further encouraging the reading process.

We feel that making reading fun and enjoyable is the single most important thing that you can do to help children become good readers. And we hope you'll be a part of Bank Street's long tradition of learning through sharing.

The Bank Street College of Education

W9-BAQ-328

For George
—M.M.

A Lucas • Evans Book

Rabbit's Birthday Kite
A Bantam Little Rooster Book
Simultaneous paper-over-board and trade paper
editions/June 1991

"Little Rooster" is a trademark of Bantam Books,
a division of Bantam Doubleday Dell Publishing Group, Inc.

Library of Congress Cataloging-in-Publication Data
Macdonald, Maryann.
Rabbit's birthday kite / by Maryann Macdonald; illustrated by
Lynn Munsinger.
p. cm.

(Bank Street ready-to-read)
"A Bantam little rooster book."
Summary: Receiving a birthday kite from Hedgehog, impatient Rabbit
learns that kite flying requires a few lessons.
ISBN 0-553-05876-2
ISBN 0-553-34908-2 (pbk.)
[1. Kites—Fiction. 2. Rabbits—Fiction. 3. Hedgehogs—Fiction.]
I. Munsinger, Lynn, ill. II. Title.
PZ7.M1486Rab   1991
[E]—dc20   89-39470
CIP
AC

Published simultaneously in the United States and Canada

Bantam Books are published by Bantam Books, a division of Bantam Dou-
bleday Dell Publishing Group, Inc. Its trademark, consisting of the words
"Bantam Books" and the portrayal of a rooster, is Registered in U.S. Patent
and Trademark Office and in other countries. Marca Registrada. Bantam
Books, 666 Fifth Avenue, New York, New York 10103.

PRINTED IN THE UNITED STATES OF AMERICA

0 9 8 7 6 5 4 3 2

Bank Street Ready-to-Read™

RABBIT'S BIRTHDAY KITE

by Maryann Macdonald
Illustrated by Lynn Munsinger

A BANTAM LITTLE ROOSTER BOOK

NEW YORK · TORONTO · LONDON · SYDNEY · AUCKLAND

Rabbit's birthday was
on a windy day in March.
Hedgehog decided to make
a kite for him.

He crossed two sticks
and tied them with string.
Then he put paper
over the sticks and string.

Last of all, he painted a picture
on the paper.
When the kite was ready,
Hedgehog set off
for Rabbit's house.

"Happy Birthday, Rabbit,"
said Hedgehog.
"A kite!" said Rabbit.

"I am going to fly it right now."
"Wait!" cried Hedgehog.
"Not here. Not yet."

But Rabbit grabbed the string.
He began to run.
"I have seen kite flying before,"
he yelled. "It's easy."
Rabbit ran as fast as he could.
The kite rose into the air.

"See?" called Rabbit.
Then the kite whirled around
and dove into a stump.
Thunk.
"Oh, no!" said Rabbit.
"My kite!"

Hedgehog ran to the kite.
"It's all right, Rabbit," he said.
"The kite isn't broken.
It just needs a tail."
"A tail?" said Rabbit,
wiggling his bottom.
"I only have one tail."

"Not that kind," said Hedgehog.
"A kite tail.
To keep it right side up."
Hedgehog and Rabbit found some rags.
They tied the longest one
to the bottom of the kite.
They tied little ones to the long one.

"Now my kite will fly," said Rabbit.
He picked up the string again
and began to run.
"Wait!" called Hedgehog.
"Not here! Not yet!"
But Rabbit did not listen.

"Don't worry, Hedgehog," he yelled.
"I have seen kite flying before.
It's easy."
The kite rose into the air.
It moved higher and a little higher.
Rabbit looked back. "See?" he said.

"Rabbit!" called Hedgehog.
"Look where you are going!"
But it was too late.
Rabbit bumped into a tree.
The kite bumped into another tree.
Hedgehog ran to his friend.
He rubbed Rabbit's bump.
"Hedgehog," said Rabbit, "I hate kites."

"I have seen kite flying before,"
he said.
"It looks so easy.
But it isn't easy for me."
"Everything is easy
once you learn how,"
said Hedgehog.

The two friends climbed up
into the tree.
The kite was bent but not torn.
It was cracked but not broken.

"Now," said Hedgehog,
"we will start over again.
We have a tail so the kite will not
whirl and crash.
We must get away from trees
so that we do not get bumped."

They walked to a grassy bluff
high above the sea.

"This is a good place to fly a kite,"
said Hedgehog.

Hedgehog held the kite,
and Rabbit held the string.
They ran together.
A strong wind lifted the kite,
and Hedgehog let go.

The kite rose into the air.
"Let out the string!"
called Hedgehog.
And Rabbit did.

The kite twisted and sailed high
into the air.
Hedgehog pulled the string.
The kite flew up to the blue sky
and the white clouds.
Rabbit pulled the string.
The kite dipped low over the sea.
The two friends sat on the bluff,
watching the kite.

"I don't hate kites anymore,"
said Rabbit.
"I know," said Hedgehog.
He took the string and pulled it.
The string snapped.
"Oh, Rabbit!" said Hedgehog.
"I am sorry!"

"Don't worry," said Rabbit.
"We can make a new kite.
You can show me how."

"That was your birthday kite!"
said Hedgehog.
"It was not that easy to make."
"Everything is easy
once you learn how," said Rabbit.

Hedgehog smiled.
"I guess you're right," he said.
And they watched the kite
fly away free, over the sea.